SOON
BABOON
SOON

dave
horowitz

G. P. PUTNAM'S SONS
NEW YORK

When I was a kid, I was sent home from school with
a note to give to my parents. The following year
I would be old enough to begin taking music lessons.
It was time to select an instrument. I circled
TROMBONE and gave the slip of paper to my parents.
They looked at the paper for a very long time.

"Wouldn't you rather play drums?" they asked.
Well, of course I would—what kid wouldn't pick drums
over some stuffy old brass instrument? Drums were not
on the list, though, likely for that very reason. My mom
added DRUMS to the bottom of the list for me to circle.
I still play almost every day.

Thanks, Mom and Dad. This performance is for you.

—D. H.

Published simultaneously in Canada.
Manufactured in China by South China Printing Co. Ltd.
Designed by Gina DiMassi. Text set in Rekord.
The art was done with cut paper, charcoal and colored pencils.
Library of Congress Cataloging-in-Publication Data
Horowitz, Dave, 1970–
Soon, Baboon, soon / by Dave Horowitz.
p. cm.   Summary: As the triangle player in the primate percussion band, Baboon has
trouble waiting patiently for his turn.   [1. Bands (Music)—Fiction. 2. Baboons—Fiction.
3. Primates—Fiction. 4. Stories in rhyme.] I. Title.   PZ8.3.H7848Soo 2005   [E]—dc22
2003024448   ISBN 0-399-24268-6   10 9 8 7 6 5 4 3 2 1
First Impression

Here comes a drummer.

Here
comes
his brother.

Here
comes
another.

He's a **drummer**
like his **brother**
and his **other brother.**

Bo

Orangutans bang every*thang.*

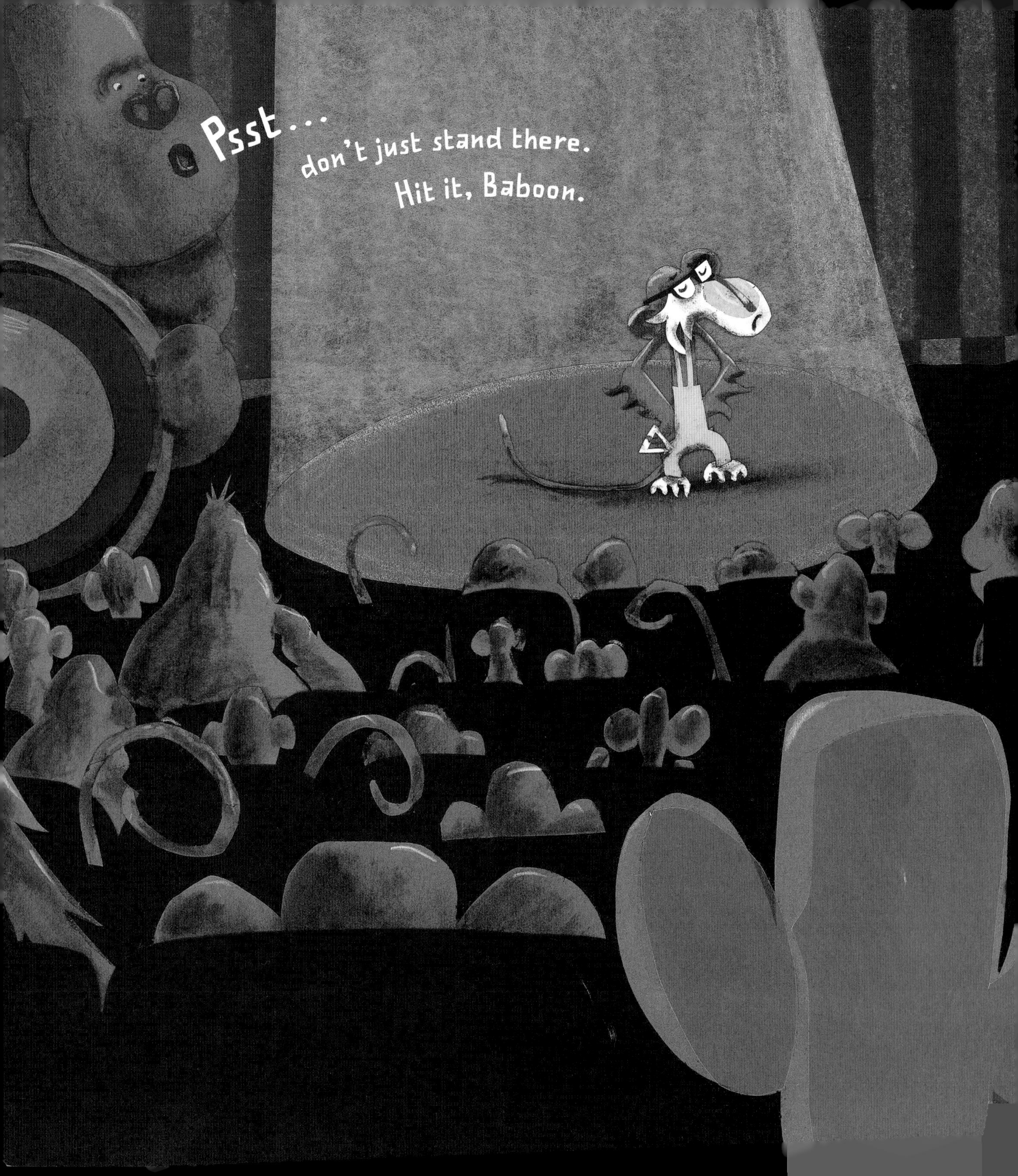
Psst...
don't just stand there.
Hit it, Baboon.

Maracas
tambourine
Trap Set
pots and pans
cans
IMWT
Marching Bass Drum
KING GONG
Gong
Ago-go bells
Timpani